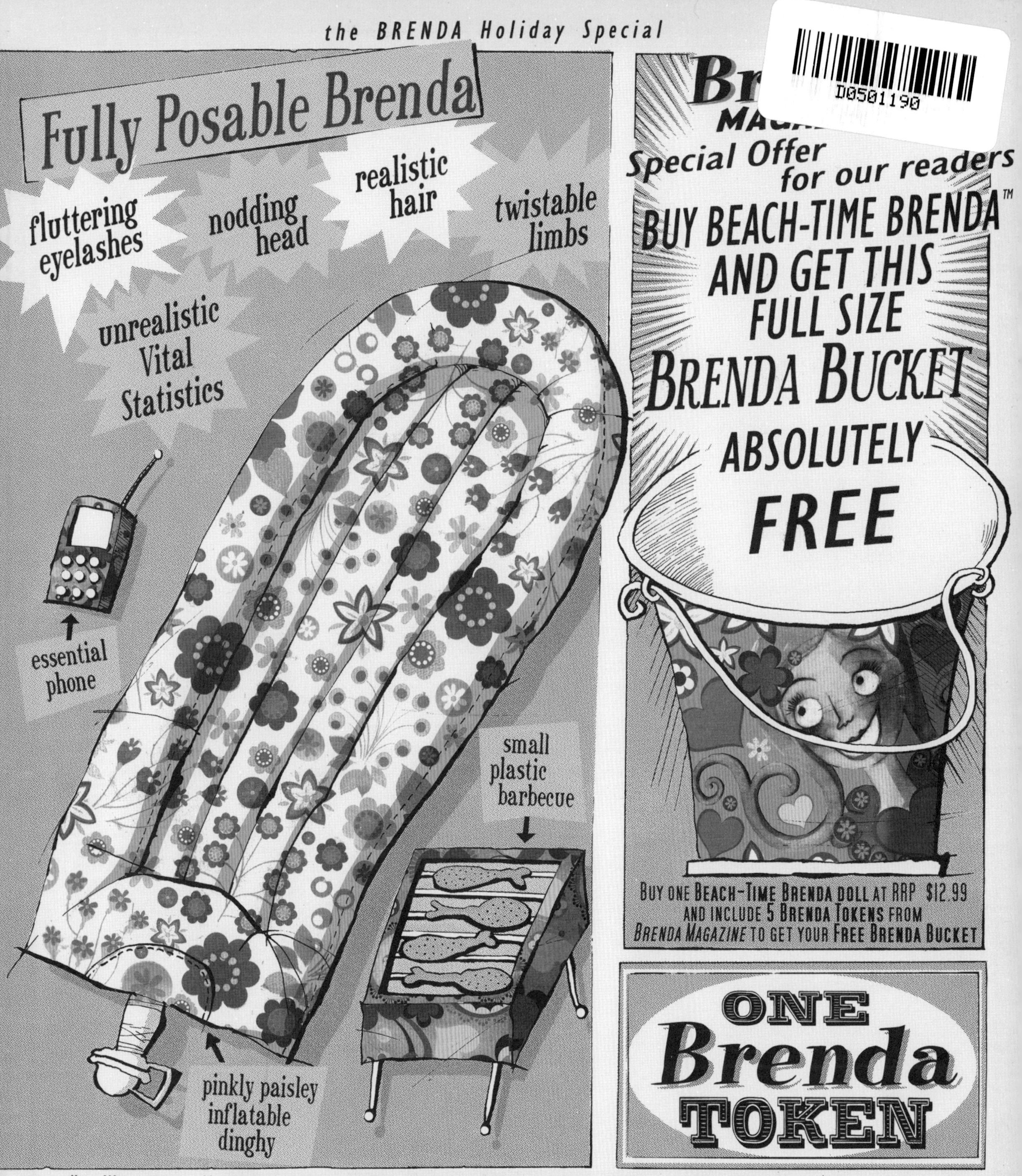
the BRENDA Holiday Special
Fully Posable Brenda
fluttering eyelashes
nodding head
realistic hair
twistable limbs
unrealistic Vital Statistics
essential phone
small plastic barbecue
pinkly paisley inflatable dinghy
Special Offer for our readers
BUY BEACH-TIME BRENDA™ AND GET THIS FULL SIZE BRENDA BUCKET ABSOLUTELY FREE
BUY ONE BEACH-TIME BRENDA DOLL AT RRP $12.99 AND INCLUDE 5 BRENDA TOKENS FROM BRENDA MAGAZINE TO GET YOUR FREE BRENDA BUCKET
ONE Brenda TOKEN
APPLY. NON-WATERPROOF - MAY DISINTEGRATE IF WET. EXTREMELY FLAMMABLE - KEEP AWAY FROM HOT SUN. WARNING: CHOKING HAZARD AND SMALL PARTS.

TRACTION MAN AND THE BEACH ODYSSEY

MINI GREY

Alfred A. Knopf New York

Everyone is going on holiday. Traction Man and his loyal pet, Scrubbing Brush, are doing an equipment check before they go.

"All there? Let's start loading, then."

Scrubbing Brush has never been on holiday before and is quite excited.

Granny's coming too. She has a new Young Pet called Truffles.

Scrubbing Brush thinks Truffles needs some Proper Training . . .

“My goodness! Look at that, Scrubbing Brush –
it must be the Wide Ocean!”

BIG AND SPARKLY
FISHSTICKS
COD 'N' HALIBUT FLAVOUR

Miranda!
QUIBBLES
Brenda
MAGAZINE
GERM
IN A BOTTLE

Traction Man and Scrubbing Brush are exploring the secret crevices of the Rockpool.

Traction Man is wearing his Squid-Proof Scuba Suit, Lightweight Shorts and Aquatic Air Tanks.

Who knows what creatures lurk in this Underwater World?

If they stay very still,
perhaps some of the
elusive Rockpool Animals
will appear.

"Here, young Prawn,
don't be shy!"

"I'd leave that well alone
if I were you,
Scrubbing Brush . . ."

"Oh dear –
too late."

LUNCHTIME!

Nearly everyone wanted to have a quick dip in the sea before lunch –

which leaves Traction Man and Scrubbing Brush and . . .

OPERATION PICNIC.

MAYO

"At all costs, this picnic must be defended against hungry Truffles."

"No, Truffles,
down, boy,
keep back
from the quiche."

Truffles seems to like Traction Man.

SLURP

"No, Truffles, that tickles – now I'm all wet."

"Hey, Truffles, put me down! Bad dog!"

DIG DIG DIG

But Truffles must think Traction Man is some sort of bone and has carried him off.

Oh no! Traction Man is being buried for later.

Don't worry, Traction Man, Scrubbing Brush has sturdy bristles and will dig you out in a jiffy.

Scrubbing Brush is doing a Victory Dance.

"Watch out behind you, Scrubbing Brush – never leave your back to the sea!"

A huge seaweed mass on a giant wave swamps Scrubbing Brush and carries him away.

Arf!

Traction Man just manages to grab on to the seaweed.

Arf!

Traction Man and Scrubbing Brush are clinging on to a plastic bottle in the vast sea.
They can hardly see land.

A colossal wave towers over them.

Traction Man is wearing quite a lot of seaweed.

W H O O S H

LIQUID GERM IN A BOTTLE

"Take a deep breath,
Scrubbing Brush,
and hold on . . ."

They are
plunged
under
the water.

It's all dark.

"Scrubbing Brush,
where are you?"

Arf!

"Thank
goodness!"

"Can you see that shape
in the gloom?

Keep very still, Scrubbing Brush,
and don't be scared
(even though it has
hot breath
and dripping jaws).

But do you hear a voice?"

What have you got there, Fluffy?

Traction Man and Scrubbing Brush are traveling by bucket . . .
a Beach-Time Brenda™ Bucket.

ICE-O
ICE-O
I don't see him anywhere, but
maybe he's been washed up
further along...

Traction Man is in the Dollies' Castle, wearing seaweed hair and beard, a shell hat, a light dusting of sand and a floral sarong.

Scrubbing Brush has been garlanded too.

The Dollies are treating them to a feast of ice cream treats.

More Raspberry Ripple,
Traction Man?
"Thank you, Ladies, but no.
One scoop is plenty."
You can stay in our castle
FOREVER!
"Somehow,
Scrubbing
Brush,
we must
escape."

. . . he's about this long,
wearing a red
scuba suit . . .
ICE-O
ICE-O

"Look there, Scrubbing Brush –
do you recognize that nose?"

Truffles!
SLURP
Truffles licks off Traction Man's seaweed beard.
My Traction Man!

"No more time for ice cream,
Ladies – Time for Action!
There seems to be
an earthquake going on
in your castle.
This structure is seriously
unstable – it's crumbling
everywhere."

Here, Traction Man,
let's deflect the rubble using this flip-flop . . .
TOFFO TO
. . . while I carry your pet to safety.

"I'm afraid your castle has been demolished by Truffles the Puppy. But don't worry, Scrubbing Brush and I can help you rebuild it in no time."

I think I see magma.
We must be nearly at the Core.
Arf!
More light in the hole, please, Scrubbing Brush!
COSTALOT COFFEE
COSTALOT COFFEE
LOLLY
WHAT'S BROWN AND STICKY?
MAN BREW
FossiL exibishuN

Traction Man, Scrubbing Brush and the Dollies
are digging an exploration hole
to the Center of the Earth.

(The Dollies are wearing Safety Jackets,
Excavation Shorts and Cave Helmets
borrowed from Traction Man.)

They have already unearthed
these buried treasures and the bones
of some ancient creature.

Behind them you can see
the Dollies' new castle.
They think it is Even Better than before.

Tomorrow they are all going to go
on an expedition to the Mysterious Cave
with their own lunch.

The Dollies have a dinghy . . .
and they are all
ready for
Anything.

Some other brilliant books by Mini Grey:

Egg Drop
The Very Smart Pea and the Princess-to-Be
Ginger Bear
Traction Man Is Here!
The Adventures of the Dish and the Spoon
Traction Man Meets Turbo Dog
Jim (by Hilaire Belloc, illustrated by Mini Grey)
Three by the Sea

THIS IS A BORZOI BOOK PUBLISHED BY ALFRED A. KNOPF

 Published in hardcover in the United States by Alfred A. Knopf, an imprint of Random House Children's Books, a division of Random House, Inc., New York. Originally published in Great Britain by Jonathan Cape, an imprint of Random House Children's Books, a division of the Random House Group Ltd, London, in 2011.

Knopf, Borzoi Books, and the colophon are registered trademarks of Random House, Inc.

Visit us on the Web! randomhouse.com/kids

Educators and librarians, for a variety of teaching tools, visit us at randomhouse.com/teachers

Library of Congress Cataloging-in-Publication Data is available upon request.

ISBN 978-0-375-86952-5 (trade) ISBN 978-0-375-96952-2 (lib. bdg.)

MANUFACTURED IN MALAYSIA

May 2012

10 9 8 7 6 5 4 3 2 1

First American Edition

Random House Children's Books supports the First Amendment and celebrates the right to read.

Dedicated to
TIA

BEACH-TIME BRENDA
IN
IT CAME FROM THE SEA
AFTER A HECTIC DAY...
...IT'S NEARLY 6 O'CLOCK AND BRENDA IS WEARING HER FLORAL PARTY SUIT AND SHIMMERING HEADSCARF. BUT ALTHOUGH HER OUTFIT IS FULLY ACCESSORIZED, HER MIND IS IN TURMOIL.
THE SNACKS AND THE SUNDOWNER COCKTAILS ARE READY – BUT WHERE ARE THE GUESTS? BRENDA IS JUST ABOUT TO GIVE UP AND RETURN TO HER HOLIDAY CHALET WHEN...
WHOOSH!
A GIANT WAVE SWEEPS IN.
TRACTION MAN!
GREAT SCOTT! I SEEM TO HAVE BEEN WASHED UP IN THE WRONG COMIC STRIP!